D0667435

PIPER MORGAN
MAKES A SPLASH

DON'T MISS ANY OF PIPER'S ADVENTURES!

Piper Morgan Joins the Circus

Piper Morgan in Charge!

Piper Morgan to the Rescue

COMING SOON:

Piper Morgan Plans a Party

ALSO BY STEPHANIE FARIS:

30 Days of No Gossip

25 Roses

MAKES A SPLASH

BY STEPHANIE FARIS

ILLUSTRATED BY LUCY FLEMING

ALADDIN

New York London Toronto Sydney New Delhi

This book is a work of fiction. Any references to historical events, real people, or real places are used fictitiously. Other names, characters, places, and events are products of the author's imagination, and any resemblance to actual events or places or persons, living or dead, is entirely coincidental.

ALADDIN
An imprint of Simon & Schuster Children's Publishing Division
1230 Avenue of the Americas, New York, New York 10020
First Aladdin hardcover edition April 2017

Also available in an Aladdin paperback edition.

For information about special discounts for bulk purchases, please contact Simon & Schuster Special Sales at 1-866-506-1949 or business@simonandschuster.com.
The Simon & Schuster Speakers Bureau can bring authors to your live event. For more information or to book an event contact the Simon & Schuster Speakers Bureau at 1-866-248-3049 or visit our website at www.simonspeakers.com.
Book designed by Laura Lyn DiSiena
The text of this book was set in New Baskerville.
Manufactured in the United States of America 0317 FFG
2 4 6 8 10 9 7 5 3 1
Library of Congress Control Number 2016963081
ISBN 978-1-4814-5718-7 (hc)
ISBN 978-1-4814-5717-0 (pbk)
ISBN 978-1-4814-5719-4 (eBook)

For Doug, the best stepdad
anyone could ask for

CHAPTER 1

It was hot outside. The perfect day to jump into a gigantic, cold pool.

Only the pool in front of me was on TV. It was part of a commercial. Before I could start daydreaming about jumping in, the camera went to a man with a big smile.

"Summer is here! It's time to buy a pool! We have inground pools, aboveground pools, hot tubs, and tanning beds!"

I pressed the minus button on the

remote control. That much noise wasn't good for anybody.

"Piper? What did I tell you about watching too much TV?" Mom asked.

I thought for a minute. I stared up at the ceiling. I think staring at the ceiling helps me think better.

"Um . . ."

I had nothing.

Mom was staring at the TV. "That's where we're going," she said, a smile slowly replacing the frown on her face. "That's my new job."

I looked at the TV. The news was on, and it was just a guy talking.

"The commercial before that," Mom said. "That's my new job."

"The pool place?" I asked, sounding shrieky as I stood up. That was the most exciting news ever. When she had talked about it earlier, it sounded like a place where they sold chairs and stuff. She didn't mention they had real pools!

My mom works lots of different jobs, but only for short times. That means I get to go on new adventures, like the circus and a school principal's office. Each adventure brought new friends!

But before we could have this next adventure, we had to get food for the week, do laundry, and help to tidy up around Nanna's house. We started staying with Nanna when Mom got a job at a school forty-five minutes away. That was lots of driving, but now Mom has a job that is only two minutes away from Nanna's house and it's at a pool place. That is just magnificent.

"Magnificent" is a new word I learned. I'm trying it out. Mag-nif-i-cent!

Mom told me I was dawdling and she wasn't "going to wait around all day, missy." Plus, she had a surprise for me. Surprises were good. Surprises maybe meant we were stopping by the clothing store that had all the purses and backpacks and jewelry.

"Come on, Oreo," I said to Nanna's dog, a little black-and-white terrier that Nanna says is a "terror." I ran down the hall to my room with Oreo on my heels. If I was really good, Mom might let me come to her new job!

Splash Fact #1

Grown-ups always say watching too much TV is bad for you. How do you know if you're watching too much TV, though? Here are some clues:

#1 You think about your favorite TV show all the time.

#2 You know more about the people you watch on TV than your own friends.

#3 You skip fun things because you don't want to miss your favorite show.

#4 You ask your mom to bring you things so you don't have to take your eyes off the screen.

#5 You compare all your friends to characters on your favorite shows.

CHAPTER 2

A couple of hours later Mom pulled the car into a big shopping plaza with a very familiar sign.

"We have inground pools, aboveground pools, hot tubs, and tanning beds!" I said, just like the man on TV had said it.

Mom looked at me funny. She stopped looking because she had to find a parking space. That meant eyes on the road.

I waited until she was all parked to ask

the question I really, really wanted to ask. It was the most important question of all the questions ever asked.

"Do you get a free pool for working here?"

Nanna had a backyard. It wasn't a big backyard, but big enough for a pool, I'll bet. I could swim all summer and Nanna and Mom could hang out by the pool and drink lemonade. Maybe I could invite

some friends to enjoy my nanna's new pool too. We could all teach Oreo how to swim. (Can dogs swim?)

All of that would be magnificent.

"No," Mom said. "But I do have a couple of surprises for you."

I smiled. I liked surprises.

There was a big truck in the parking lot that had the word PRODUCTION on the side. A guy standing next to it had a black T-shirt that read CREW.

"What's that?" I asked as we walked toward the building.

Mom looked over. "Hmm. They must be shooting a commercial today or something. How exciting for you!"

I bounced up and down a little as I walked. A real TV commercial. Maybe they'd put me in it, and I could become a

TV star! I could yell, “We have inground pools, aboveground pools, hot tubs, and tanning beds!” better than anyone in the whole wide world.

I didn’t see the cameras at first, but while Mom was talking to the woman behind the counter, I saw them! They weren’t that far away, either. And best of all—they were moving.

“We also have all the pool liners and supplies you need,” another man said to the camera. I knew the voice. That was the guy from the TV commercial.

Now was my chance to be super famous. I just had to show them what I had. They’d move the camera to me and everyone would see me for just that second.

“We have inground pools, aboveground pools, hot tubs, and tanning beds!”

I said the words as loudly as I could. I was also walking toward the camera as I said it, putting me right behind the man who had been talking. He was now looking at me. And so was the camera.

"Hi!" I said cheerily, waving and smiling my biggest smile. "I'm Piper Morgan."

Someone behind me gasped. It was my mom. She was standing there staring at me, and I knew that look on her face.

She was not happy.

Splash Fact #2

Most people think all dogs can swim. That's what "doggy paddle" means, after all. Throw a dog in a pool and he'll start moving his legs, right?

Wrong.

Some dogs can swim without even being taught. They just *know*. Some dogs might not know what to do when they first are in water, but they can learn. And some dogs would just sink to the bottom if you didn't hold them up.

If you aren't sure which one your dog is, have your mom or dad hold your dog up in the water to see what he does. If he's a natural swimmer, you'll know pretty soon.

Family Center
Super swim

CHAPTER 3

My mom was mad at me because I didn't "show responsibility, young lady." And that's bad.

I'm not so good at the "responsibility" thing, even though I try really hard. Just when I show my mom I can be the most responsible seven-year-old girl ever, I mess up.

"Am I going to work with you?" I asked Mom as I climbed into the backseat. She had told me to wear my bathing suit under my clothes, so I was hoping that meant I would be helping out somehow. It was the next morning after the "fiasco" at the pool store. That's what my mom called it. See, when I yelled out to the camera, they were live. That meant people who were watching the morning news saw me on TV.

I was excited about that, but I couldn't let my mom know.

"No," Mom said. "You're going to a place where you'll hopefully get rid of some of that energy you have."

We pulled up to a building with a sign that read FAMILY CENTER. Mom was going to work, so it couldn't be for "family," whatever we were doing. It would just be me.

"Is it a daycare?" I asked Mom. "Will there be other kids there?"

"Yes," Mom said. "Well, sort of. We're signing you up for the 'guppies' program. You'll get to learn to be a guppy."

A guppy was a fish. I knew that because I'd had a book about fish when I was a little kid.

Wait. Did that mean I would have to get in the water like a fish too? Even though I loved the idea of a pool, I didn't know how to swim yet.

I wanted to ask more questions, but Mom was in "I mean business" mode. When she's like that, she doesn't really hear me. She just says words like "uh-huh" and "I see," which mean, "You may as well be talking to the wall."

"Which way to the guppies sign-up?" Mom asked the smiley girl at the entrance.

The girl pointed to the left. "Are you

excited about being a guppy?" she asked me.

Mom had my hand, though, and she was tugging on it as she walked away. So I just gave the girl a funny look and ran after my mom. *That wasn't very nice,* I thought. I wanted to go back and be nice and ask what a guppy was.

But in front of us was a small group of kids, all standing in a crowd. There were two boys and three girls.

Their parents were in a line. I wanted to hang with the kids.

"Go ahead," Mom said, before I could even ask.

I ran straight to the group, slowing down as I got closer. I didn't want to scare them. "I'm Piper!" I announced. They were all looking at me, so what else could I say?

"Are you a guppy?" one of the girls asked.

"I don't know," I said. "I think so. What does a guppy do?"

"Swim," one of the boys said.

Oh no. "I can't," I said. "I don't know how."

I waited for them to laugh at me. But they didn't laugh at all.

"We can't swim either," one of the girls said. "That's what a guppy is. We're learn-to-swimmers."

"Learn-to-swimmers." I liked that!

"Mom!" I said, turning to look at her. She was talking to a woman in line. A responsible guppy wouldn't keep yelling at her when she was busy, busy, busy. So I turned back and talked to my new friends. We would all be guppies together.

And maybe . . . if I showed Mom that I could be a good, "responsible" swimmer, I could help her out at the pool place after all!

Splash Fact #3

Did you know there are different kinds of swimming pools? Some you can have in your own backyard. Some you have to pay to swim in. How many of these pools have you swam in?

#1 Aboveground pools. These pools aren't very big, but they're perfect for families! None of the pool goes below the ground.

#2 Inground pools. These are the kinds of pools that go in a hole in the ground. Many residences and families have these!

#3 Olympic-size pools. Most homes don't have these. They're really big! A lot of athletes use these to do laps and train for their sport. A lot of public pools are Olympic size too.

CHAPTER 4

There were six people in my swim class. Two of the girls, Erin and Annabelle, were my favorites. Erin was going on vacation and wanted to know how to swim first. And Annabelle's family just got a new pool.

"My mom works at the pool place!" I said when I heard that. "They sell inground pools, aboveground pools, hot tubs, and tanning beds!"

Erin and Annabelle didn't know about that commercial. But that was okay. I told them my big news.

"They were on TV and I was there," I said. "I yelled out, 'I'm Piper Morgan!'"

"Wow, you're famous!" Erin exclaimed.

"That's great!" Annabelle added.

"Only my mom wasn't happy," I said, frowning. "She says I'm not 'responsible.'"

"'Cause you were on TV?" Annabelle asked. "That's silly."

"I know!" I was so excited that someone else thought it was silly. "She said I shouldn't have interrupted the commercial."

"You weren't supposed to be in the commercial?" Erin asked.

"Well . . . no," I admitted.

Erin and Annabelle looked at each other. They didn't look too impressed anymore.

"I didn't mean to do it," I told them. "It just slipped out."

That was true. When I saw the cameras, I just blurted out the line from the commercial. Just like I had when I heard Annabelle had a new pool.

They looked at each other again, but this time they nodded. They were on my side, I could tell. I liked that.

"I just have to be a really good swimmer," I said. "Then my mom will let me work at the pool place with her."

"And maybe you can be in a commercial," Annabelle said. "Everyone likes commercials with kids in them."

We had to practice going underwater then, so I didn't get to talk to my friends anymore. But I thought about what Annabelle said. A commercial would be

the best thing ever. It would be even better than being on live TV for a second, because it would play over and over and over and over again.

Mom was really proud of me, she said when she picked me up after swimming class to take me back to Nanna's.

"Am I showing responsibility?" I asked, hoping, hoping, *hoping* she'd say yes.

"Yes, you are," Mom said with a laugh.

"Can I go back to the pool place with you tomorrow?" I asked. "I'll be really good. I promise."

"Maybe," she said. "We'll see how you do tonight with taking your bath and getting to bed on time."

That was no problem at all. I liked taking my bath, although sometimes I stayed in the tub until my fingertips got all wrinkly. I also liked going to bed, but only if I could read my book first. Tonight I wouldn't beg to read just one more chapter. When Mom said, "Lights out," I'd say, "Okay."

"Are they going to do a new commercial for your pool place?" I asked Mom as we pulled into Nanna's driveway.

Mom gave me a funny look. For a second I thought she might have figured out I wanted to be on TV again. It was a scary second. I was smart, though.

"Just 'cause I'm tired of seeing the other one," I said quickly. "I think they should do a new one."

"Maybe you're right," she said. "They're doing a new commercial very soon, as a matter of fact. We'll have to watch TV until we see it come on."

I smiled. I had to be the most responsible seven-year-old ever to make sure Mom let me be in the commercial. My plan would work, I was sure of it!

Splash Fact #4

Have you ever seen your favorite TV star on a commercial? Those are called "spokespeople." Companies pay famous people lots of money to shoot a thirty-second commercial saying nice things about their products.

Sometimes you don't even see famous people on a commercial. You just hear their voices. And then it bugs you for days and days because you can't figure out where you've heard that voice before.

Most of the time the people you see on commercials aren't famous at all. But they get to be on TV. Which kind of makes them famous.

CHAPTER 5

I followed Mom into the pool place, my backpack bouncing against my back as I moved. I was walking behind Mom, but not fast enough. She had to keep stopping and wait for me to catch up.

Mom was late. It wasn't my fault. I was ready with lots of minutes left. She'd been on the phone with the recruiter for a long time and she didn't want to be rude. She almost left me at home with Nanna because "there's not enough time," but I'd said "please, please, please, please" until she knew she'd be even later if she kept arguing with me.

Mom walks really fast when she's late. She walks fast when she's not late too, but even faster when she's late.

I moved my legs as fast as I could, but I had to run to keep up with her. Finally we got to the front door and she rushed inside, letting me run in behind her. I was hoping she'd forget about me and I could go play, but nope.

"You'll be in here until lunch, and then I'll take you home," Mom said, leading me into an office near the front of the store. "Just do your summer reading and be really, really quiet, okay?"

"Then can I tour the store?" I ask. "If

I'm quiet, can I help you work?"

"We'll see," she said, closing the door behind her.

"We'll see" is something grown-ups say when they don't want to say no just yet. "We'll see" always becomes no. Don't ever believe "we'll see."

Mom left and went off to do her work. I looked around the office. This wasn't what today was supposed to be. My mom worked at a pool place. I wanted to look at all the awesome pools and hot tubs and stuff. I wanted to help her work.

I sat in my chair with my backpack still on. I grabbed a book. I opened it. I stared at the words. That lasted about three seconds before I looked up at the door.

There were pools on the other side of that door. One had water in it. I'd seen

POOL STUFF
Shark!

it with my very own two eyes. I also had my bathing suit in my backpack. I could change into it and maybe talk Mom into letting me swim. Since there weren't any customers around, she probably wouldn't mind, right? I could even demonstrate some of the pools to customers and maybe make them want to buy them. That would make me the best pool store worker ever.

I changed into my *cutest ever* bathing suit with the polka dots all over. I couldn't swim without something to hold me up, though. I walked to the door and looked through the window. There they were—the answers to all my questions. Hanging from the ceiling were inner tubes. I just had to get one of those. There were probably some on the floor somewhere.

I opened the door, looked both ways,

and sneaked out. I didn't see any other people, but I knew I had to get to where nobody could see me. A little girl running around in her bathing suit would be hard to miss.

I ran straight for the big, tall shelves and hid between two of them. Then I started looking for inner tubes. Or anything that could help me float. I couldn't swim on my own yet, but that would be okay. Mom would see me in the pool and know I was all grown up now.

There were no floaty things anywhere. I didn't understand why. I sneaked to more shelves the next aisle over. On my third aisle, I found a stack of inner tubes. Only they were all flat.

I'd have to blow one up. Like a balloon. Mom always said I was "full of hot air," so

stock
$1 80
NO SWIMMING
Inner Tube

maybe that would help. I opened the little plastic thing, took a deep breath, and started blowing.

It only budged a little. Then a little more. But it seemed like every time I stopped to take a breath, some of the air came back out again. I was getting nowhere.

I needed a blower-upper thing. They had them at the swimming pool where I took lessons with the other Guppies. I saw the lifeguards use it sometimes when one of the inner tubes was too flimsy. I kept blowing into the tube while I walked around looking.

There it was! I saw it! It was a hosey-thing over by one of the pools. All I had to do was push the hose up to the inner tube and air would come out.

I walked over to the hose, which was

hanging over the top of one of the pools. I pulled on it and reached for my inner tube. I yanked and yanked and finally it came out of the pool. Too fast. The entire hose came out at once.

That was when I saw it wasn't a hose at all. It was the vacuum thing that the lifeguards at my swimming pool used to suck up dirt. One of them had shown us how it worked just a couple of days ago.

"Ahhhh," I yelled. I tripped and fell backward right into the pool, bringing a long pole crashing to the ground with a loud *thud.*

The store had seemed empty before, but now it seemed like people came from everywhere. All of a sudden lots and lots of people were staring at me. And they did not look happy.

Splash Fact #5

Did you know at one time there was no such thing as a bathing suit? Then they started making laws that you had to wear something if you were going to swim.

At first, bathing suits for women were long dresses. They were made so that you couldn't see through them when they were wet.

During the 1900s bathing suits started showing arms and legs. Some people didn't like that style at first, but they probably remembered that it was really hot outside. And nobody wants to be on the beach in a long-sleeved dress when it's hot outside. Now there are all kinds of bathing suits to choose from for both men and women!

CHAPTER 6

Mom and I drove home in silence. I could tell Mom was thinking about how "not" responsible I was the entire ride.

After dinner Nanna waited until Mom had left the room to ask what had happened at the pool shop. I'd been mostly quiet as I ate, while Mom and Nanna talked about boring grown-up stuff. But the second Mom had gone to the bathroom, Nanna moved in.

"What happened?" she whispered.

"There was a pool vacuum," I said. "I knocked it over and fell in the pool. Mom got upset."

"Was it by accident?" Nanna asked.

I thought about that for a second. I didn't knock the vacuum over on purpose. But it wasn't really an accident.

"I needed an inner tube," I explained. "They were all flat."

I pressed my palms together to show her what "flat" meant.

"Why did you need an inner tube?" Nanna asked. "Were you playing?"

"I wanted to swim," I said.

Nanna gasped. "Swim?" she asked. "At your mom's work?"

"Yes," I said. "It's a pool shop."

Maybe she'd forgotten that part.

"Piper, you don't swim at a pool shop," she explained. "The pools don't even have water in them, do they?"

"Just one," I said. "I saw it."

"You do understand why it wouldn't be a smart idea to do that, though, right?"

I thought about that one. Nanna was right. Someone who was "responsible" wouldn't sneak into a pool to swim. It was dangerous. Plus, it could get Mom in trouble with her boss.

"It wasn't very responsible," I admitted. "I should say I'm sorry to Mom and her boss."

"You should," Nanna agreed. "But you should do more than that. You should prove to your mom that you're going to try really hard to do better."

I sighed. I was supposed to already be

showing that I was trying hard. Now I had to start all over again.

I'd never be on TV again at this rate.

Splash Fact #6

Some kids like to take a bath. Some kids don't. But in the 1900s people took baths about once a week. The bathtub was in the kitchen, where moms heated up water on the fire to make bathwater.

Most families had bath time on Saturday night. Many dads worked all week and took Sundays off, so Saturday nights were for getting clean. The whole family usually took a bath in the same bathwater.

Think about that the next time your parents ask you if you've taken a bath or shower today.

CHAPTER 7

"My nanna says it wasn't a very responsible thing to do," I told Erin and Annabelle at swim practice the next day. Our swim teacher was running a little late, so we were chatting until he arrived.

"It kinda wasn't," Erin said, wrapping her fluffy blue towel around her arms. "You shouldn't have grabbed the hose without an adult around."

"There were lots of adults around," I

protested. "There were managers and employees all over the place."

"There were?" Annabelle asked.

"Well . . . there would have been once I was in the pool," I said.

I frowned. Now that I was telling my new BFFs about it, it didn't make much sense. All I'd wanted to do was get a tube and show what I could do with it. I didn't think for a second about what could go wrong.

"Now I have to show my mom I can be responsible," I said. "And I have to do it fast. The TV commercial starts filming this week sometime, I think."

"This week?" Erin asked.

"That's too soon," Annabelle said. "You need more time."

"I don't have it," I said.

There would be more commercials, I knew. But we might be at a different job by that time. If I wanted to be in a TV commercial, it had to be *now.*

"You have to be at the store when they're there," Annabelle said. "That's the first step."

"Yep," Erin said. "And you wait for your perfect chance. It'll happen."

"But you have to figure out a way to get your mom to take you to work first," Annabelle pointed out. "And you have to do it fast."

"My mom always likes it when I help Nanna clean up after dinner," I said. "And take my bath without being told. And go to bed without asking to read just one more chapter."

"Do that," Erin said. "But more, too.

Help your mom with . . . other mom things."

"I help clean the house sometimes," Annabelle suggested. "My mom really likes that."

I thought about that. My new friends were right. If I showed how hard I could work at home, my mom would see that I would be a great helper at the pool shop. Then I could go and be a good little girl and maybe they'd put me in the commercial.

I smiled to myself. I liked my new plan. My new friends were the best!

Splash Fact #7

Making a TV commercial isn't easy. It takes a lot of people to put together what you see on TV. Here are a few things you have to do if you want to get a commercial on TV:

#1 Come up with a great idea: something that people will like and want to buy!

#2 Get someone to write it. This person should be good enough to come up with interesting things to say about your awesome idea!

#3 Hire a great spokesperson who loves your idea and will tell everyone about it!

CHAPTER
★ 8 ★

On Wednesdays Nanna plays old-people cards. It's called "peanut-cul" or something like that. I wanted to ask if they eat lots of peanuts while they're playing, but I was trying to be super, super, *super* good.

Nanna's card game was good news for me because that means she couldn't watch me while Mom went to work, since it was summer. Mom didn't have a babysitter for me yet, and swim lessons weren't on Wednesdays. Plus, I was being extra good. She *had* to take me to work.

"Oh my!" Nanna said when she came into the bathroom and saw me shining the knobs on the sink with a paper towel. I couldn't find the window cleaner stuff, so I was doing it with water. "You are on quite a cleaning spree, young lady."

I didn't know what a "spree" was, but that sounded like a good thing. Mom watched me last night after dinner while I helped clean up after and put all my toys away. I even took Oreo out for walks last night and this morning.

"I think I know what this is all about," Nanna said. "You want to be on that TV commercial, right?"

I stopped wiping. "How did you know about the commercial?" I asked.

"Your mom told me," Nanna said.

Uh-oh. Mom knew I wanted to be in the commercial? And she told Nanna? That wasn't a good thing.

"Your mom said there was another commercial this week," Nanna said. "And you were so interested in going to work with her. I put two and two together."

"And that equals four," I announced proudly.

"Yes, it does," Nanna said, laughing.

"I've been really responsible like you said," I told her. "Do you think Mom will take me?"

Nanna came over to stand next to me, leaning against the counter. "If she does,

do you know what that means?" she asked.

I was pretty sure I did, but I wanted to hear what Nanna would say.

"You have to be extra good," she said. "The kind of good you've been here, only the opposite. Instead of running around cleaning and doing things, you have to sit really still where she tells you to sit. And you need to do your summer reading and not sneak off, even if there are TV cameras."

I swallowed, but it felt like there was a knot in my throat. Nanna was right. If I went to work with Mom, I couldn't be in the commercial. I had to be a good girl like I was supposed to be. I could feel my dreams of being on TV disappearing while I stood there.

"I understand," I said, nodding.

And that was when I realized something. If there was a choice between staying with a babysitter and not being in the commercial or going to work with Mom and not being in the commercial, I'd pick going to work with Mom. I wanted to go to work with Mom to show her I was a big girl. You know why?

Because that was why I wanted to be in

the TV commercial. So Mom would see me on TV and be proud of me. But I just now figured out that she'd be prouder of me if I was good and did what she wanted. And she wouldn't be proud of me if I jumped into the commercial and was on TV for it.

So I'd go to work with Mom. I'd be good. And maybe I would never, ever be in a commercial, and I was A-okay with that.

Splash Fact #8

Lifeguards know how to keep people safe around water.

When you go to the pool, you probably see lifeguards sitting on those high-up seats and think, *That looks like an easy job.* It's not. Lifeguards are super strong and have to watch for someone who needs to be saved. When they see that, they have to be quick.

Lifeguards do more out of the water too. They blow the whistle at kids who run, because we could fall and hurt ourselves. They can also help with sunburns and wounds—in case you do fall while you're running by the pool.

It's important to keep us safe while having fun!

Fairy Tales

CHAPTER 9

I didn't mind reading. I had lots and lots of books to read. Mom would be proud of me if I read all the books in my backpack. That would show I was super responsible.

I was sitting behind a very big desk in the middle of the sales floor. That was more fun than the little room, and it meant the salespeople could keep an eye on me. One saleswoman named Judy kept me company when she didn't have customers. She even brought me water when I looked thirsty.

From here I could see the TV commercial being filmed, even though it was happening way on the other side of the store. Judy was watching me watch the cameras and people over there. She watched me for a long time before she got an idea.

"Can you take this to Mr. Rapp?" Judy asked. She was holding up a cup of water.

I frowned. "Who is Mr. Rapp?"

"The guy with the tie," she said, pointing to the commercial people.

Mr. Rapp was the yelly guy from the TV commercial. The guy who said they have inground pools, aboveground pools, hot tubs, and tanning beds!

"Are you sure it's okay?" I asked. "My mom told me to sit right here and not to move."

Judy smiled. "Of course, it's okay," she said. "You're saving me a trip all the way over there. I need to keep an eye on things. I'll watch you the whole time."

I took the water and walked carefully toward the commercial people. I didn't want to trip on anything or knock anything over. That wouldn't be something a responsible young lady did.

"Okay, ready to go?" I heard some woman saying as I got closer. "One more time, from the top. Ready in three, two, one!"

That was when Mr. Rapp started talking. He spoke fast and excitedly, like I spoke when I was telling Mom a story about school. It didn't even sound like he took a breath in between each sentence.

"Cut!" the woman shouted when the yelly guy was in the middle of a sentence.

"This isn't working. Something's off."

I didn't get it. It sounded good to me.

"Let's break for five," the woman said. "I need to think."

I made a frowny face at the woman's back as she turned to walk away. Then I remembered why I was there. I turned back to the tie guy, who also had a frowny face.

"You're Piper, right?" the man said. "I'm Mr. Rapp."

He knew my name? I wondered why.

"Yup, that's me!" I said. "And I have water for you."

I held out the cup. The man didn't take it. He just laughed.

"You're quite a little charmer," he said. "Maybe *you* should do this commercial."

I started to get all excited about that, but then I remembered I was just here

to hand over water. That was it.

"You do it better," I said. Then I imitated his voice, yelling, "We have inground pools, aboveground pools, hot tubs, and tanning beds!"

That brought a big laugh from the man. "Yes, I remember when you said that live on the air last week," he said. "You wouldn't believe how many people come in here asking about the little girl from TV."

I pulled the water back toward me, since he wasn't going to take it. "People ask about me?"

"Sure," he said. "That's why you'd be the perfect person to save this commercial. Valerie?"

The woman who had walked away suddenly reappeared. She was talking into her phone and looking annoyed.

"This is Piper Morgan," he said. "She has something to say."

He nudged my back. I thought for a second and finally figured out what he wanted me to do.

"We have inground pools, aboveground pools, hot tubs, and tanning beds!" I shouted with all the enthusiasm I could muster.

The woman named Valerie said, "I have to call you back," into the phone, then shoved it into her pocket. "I think we can work with this," she said with a smile. "What's your name?"

"Piper Morgan."

"Is your mom around?" she asked.

I looked at Mr. Rapp. What if telling

him who my mom was got me fired? But I had to tell the truth. Not only because telling fibs always got me in trouble, but because to be in a commercial, they'd need my mom.

"Her mom works here," Mr. Rapp said. "Could you go get Ms. Morgan?"

He said that to a guy standing nearby, who nodded and rushed off. I didn't want to get in trouble with Mom. I was just delivering water and this happened!

By the time the guy returned with Mom, my heart was beating super fast. It felt like it might pound right out of my chest. I took deep breaths and gave Mom my best "this isn't my fault at all" look.

"Your little girl was kind enough to bring me some water," Mr. Rapp said.

"Judy told me to!" I told Mom.

"Piper, don't interrupt," Mom said.

I pressed my lips tight so no more words could come out.

"And we were just won over by her charm," Mr. Rapp continued. "Valerie and I were thinking she might be the perfect person for our commercial."

Mom looked from Mr. Rapp to me. I couldn't tell if she was upset or happy. She was making no faces at all.

"Piper, may I speak with you a second?" Mom asked.

Uh-oh. That probably meant I was in trouble. I had experience with speaking with Mom for a second. Lots of experience.

We went over to the corner, where Mr. Rapp and Valerie and the other TV people couldn't hear us. Mom leaned over to be closer to me.

"Do you want to be in the commercial?" she asked.

I nodded very hard. "Yes!" I added, just in case the nod wasn't enough.

"And are you going to be careful and do what they say?"

Again I nodded and said yes at the same time.

"Okay," she said with a big grin. "Let's go make this happen."

Splash Fact #9

All you have to do is look around the pool to see that kids swim more than grown-ups. But it's important to know how to swim. Here are a few fun facts about swimming:

#1 ALMOST HALF OF AMERICA CAN'T SWIM.

#2 THE FASTEST HUMAN CAN SWIM ABOUT TWO METERS PER SECOND, WHICH EQUALS ABOUT 1.5 MILES PER HOUR.

#3 THE WHITE HOUSE HAS ONLY HAD AN OUTDOOR SWIMMING POOL SINCE 1975. PRESIDENT GERALD FORD ADDED IT.

CHAPTER 10

I thought I'd know when my commercial was going to be on TV the first time. They'd call and tell us or something. They didn't.

We finished the commercial, and a couple of weeks later, there it was. It just came on while I was getting ready for swim class. I heard Mr. Rapp's voice and came running.

"It's on! It's on!"

I yelled those words as loud as I could and still wasn't as loud as Mr. Rapp. That meant Mom couldn't hear me. So I yelled louder.

"What's all the yelling about?" Nanna asked as she came running in from the kitchen.

"What on earth?" Mom yelled as she came rushing from the back bedrooms.

I just pointed at the TV. Mr. Rapp was walking around, pointing at things. He would get to me any second now—

"There I am!" I yelled, pointing at the screen. "I'm on!"

"Okay, okay," Mom said, but she was smiling as she looked at the screen.

"Come join Piper and me and pick out your new pool for the summer," Mr. Rapp said. I ran over, just like I was supposed

to, and stood by one of the big pools in the showroom.

And then it was over.

"Did you see?" I asked Mom and Nanna. I was already looking for the remote to watch it again.

"I saw," Nanna said.

"So did I," Mom said. She smiled. "You did a great job. We're really proud of you, Piper."

"I'm going to put something online about it," Nanna said. "I can't wait to tell all the women in my book club."

She rushed off. I looked at Mom, grinning. "Can we stay here?" I asked. "I like working at the pool store." I liked hanging out with Erin and Annabelle during the swim classes too!

"Piper, you know the pool store is just

temporary," Mom said gently. "They just need extra help for summer. We'll be doing something new soon."

I thought about that for a second. I liked Mr. Rapp and all the pools, but there weren't any young people at the pool store. It wasn't my favorite of all my mom's jobs. Maybe we'd do something even better.

"What do you think about throwing parties," Mom said. "That might be fun, right?"

"Can we still stay with Nanna?" I asked. I loved being with Nanna and Oreo.

"We'll see," Mom said. "If not, we'll have a new adventure, right?"

I smiled. That was exactly what I'd been thinking.

Don't miss Piper's
next adventure:

PIPER MORGAN PLANS A PARTY

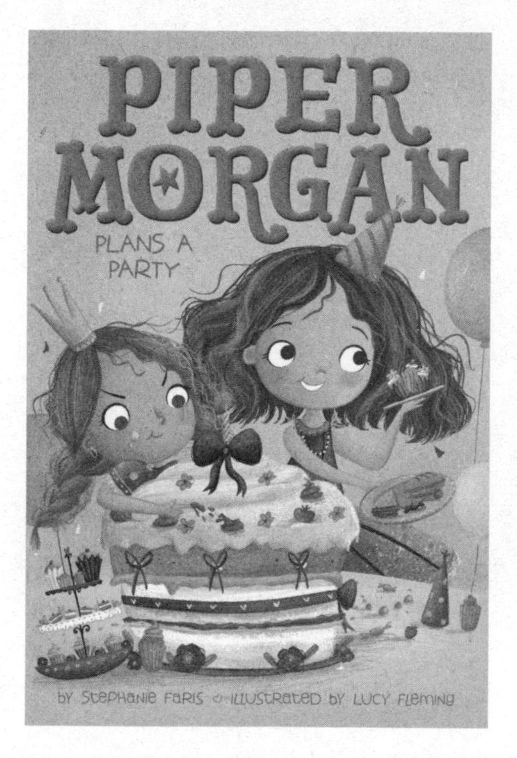